S0-EKO-945

Many Names for Eileen

Many Names for
Eileen

PEGGY SULLIVAN

ILLUSTRATED BY
MURIEL WOOD

FOLLETT PUBLISHING COMPANY
CHICAGO   **F**   NEW YORK

Text copyright © 1969 by Peggy Sullivan. Illustrations copyright © 1969 by Follett Publishing Company. All rights reserved. No portion of this book may be reproduced in any form without written permission from the publisher. Manufactured in the United States of America. Published simultaneously in Canada by The Ryerson Press, Toronto.

SBN 695-45521-4 Titan binding
SBN 695-85521-2 Trade binding

Library of Congress Catalog Card Number: 68-10485

First Printing
J

For all the people who said,
"Keep writing!"

... and ...

especially for
my niece of many names

Time to get up, Missy," Mother called.

Eileen hopped out of bed, got dressed, and ran into the kitchen. Mother was pouring white milk.

"Oh, Mommy, it's Saturday, and I want chocolate milk. You promised," Eileen said.

"That's right, honey, I did. You run out and ask the milkman for some. Tell him I forgot to leave a note."

Eileen ran out to the sidewalk just as the milkman was getting into his truck. He waved at her and waited. He smiled down at her when he handed her the milk, and he said, "Okay, Curlytop, there's your chocolate milk. Don't drop it!"

"My name's Eileen," Eileen said, but the milkman drove away.

When she was drinking her chocolate milk,
Eileen said to Mother, "The milkman knows my
name. Why does he call me Curlytop?"

"Because your hair curls all over the top of
your head—and you haven't even combed it,"
Mother told her. Eileen didn't think that was a
very good reason, but she didn't say so. Mother
said, "And I guess there's another reason, but I'll
tell you that some other time."

Now what could that reason be, Eileen wondered as she ate her breakfast.

The doorbell rang while she was still eating, and Eileen went to the door. The mailman said, "Does a princess live here? I have a package for her."

"Princess! That's me!" Eileen answered. She took the package and closed the door. Then she opened the door and said, "Thank you. And my name's Eileen."

"Okay, Princess," the mailman said as he walked away.

"Look, Mommy! A package from Grampa
and Gramma! For me! I know it's for me because it says it's for Princess, and that's what
Grampa calls me. I think it's a book. Can I open
it right now?"

Mother brought her scissors to cut the twine
on the package, and Eileen opened it. It *was* a

book, a wonderful book with a picture on each page, along with the first letter of the word for the picture. Eileen turned each page and saw an automobile, a bed, a castle, a dog—and just about in the middle, a princess. She looked up and asked, "Mommy, why does Grampa call me Princess?"

"Because he used to call me Princess, I guess."

"You? A princess?" Eileen laughed. "But why did he do that?"

"For the same reason the milkman calls you Curlytop," Mother said.

"The milkman calls me Curlytop because my hair curls all over the top of my head."

"Oh, I mean the other reason," Mother answered. "Now go and comb that curly hair on top of your head."

Eileen looked at herself in the mirror as she combed her hair. It would be nice to be a princess. It would be nice to live in a castle. But in a castle she wouldn't ever see a milkman or have a

good neighbor like Vicky. She wanted to show Vicky her new book.

Vicky liked the new book, but she wanted to look at it all by herself. So she said, "Eileen, you can go look at our baby while he's taking his nap, if you'll let me look at the book."

Eileen went upstairs very quietly, and tiptoed into the baby's bedroom. But he wasn't asleep. He was reaching for some plastic butter-flies flying above his bed, and he was smiling. When he saw her, he smiled even more. "I-ee," he said, "I-ee."

Eileen stood close to him and put out a finger for him to hold. His soft, damp hand closed on it, and he said, "I-ee, I-ee."

"Ei-leen. Say Ei-leen," Eileen whispered to him.

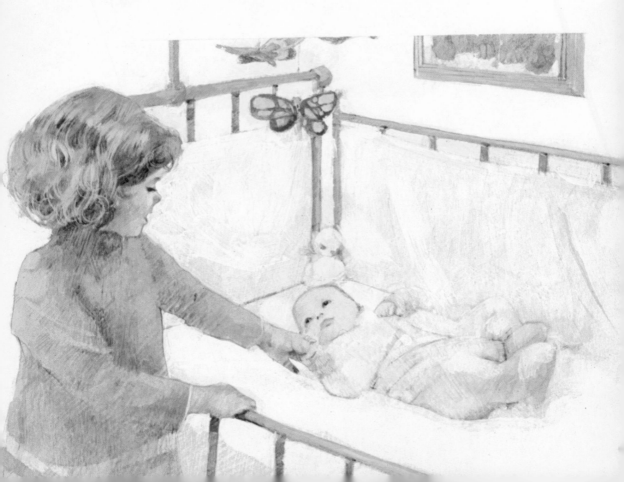

"He knows your name!" Vicky said from the doorway. She had followed Eileen up after all. "He won't even try to say Vicky."

"He says I-ee, but I want him to say Eileen. I suppose that's pretty good for a baby, though."

When she went home and her mother asked how the baby was, Eileen told her he had tried to say her name. "But he can't say Eileen. He just says I-ee. Do you know why?"

"Give him time," Mother said. "He's just a baby, and he doesn't know any words at all, really."

"And is it maybe because of that other reason, too?" Eileen asked. "That secret reason?"

"That may be part of it." And that was all Mother would say.

Ella's birthday was the next day. Ella was Eileen's other grandmother. Eileen was going to write her own birthday card and wrap her own gift, so she had to practice. Over and over, on several pieces of paper, she wrote, "Happy birthday to Ella from Little Ella."

Mother was sitting in the living room when Eileen showed her her best writing. Eileen said, "Little Ella. That's me. Little Ella means Eileen, doesn't it?"

"Yes, it does, because it's Irish."

"And I'm named after Ella?"

"That's right."

"And I'm just like Ella?"

"That's what everybody says. You look like Ella, you walk like Ella, and you like to ride ponies just like Ella used to like to ride horses. Yes, you are very much like Ella."

"So she calls me Little Ella. I like that, but my name is Eileen."

"That's right."

"Mommy, does she call me Little Ella for that secret reason, too?"

"Yes, I'm sure she does."

"Do you think I could ever guess that reason?"

"Oh, I don't think so."

Curlytop, Princess, I-ee, Little Ella—they were nice names, but there were so many of them. Eileen wanted somebody to call her Eileen. And just then, somebody did.

"Eileen!" Daddy called to her from the driveway. He had had the car washed, and now he was home and waiting for her. Eileen ran out to the car. They were going to go to the pony ring.

They drove off, and Eileen told Daddy how much Vicky had liked her new book and how the baby had tried to say her name.

Daddy smiled as he listened. "You like babies, Tiger?"

"Oh, Daddy, please don't call me Tiger."

"But that's your name."

Daddy was teasing her, so she said, "No, it's not. My name's Eileen. You know that!"

"And your other name—*my* name for you —is Tiger," Daddy said.

"Where did you ever get that name for me?" Eileen asked.

"*You* know. When you were a baby, you didn't cry very much at all, and you never whined. But once in a while, you would let out a roar like a tiger. Isn't that a good reason?"

"But there's another reason, isn't there?"

"Oh, yes, you had a little brown and yellow suit and you looked like a tiger in it. Does that make it all right?"

"I guess those are pretty good reasons. But do you know of a secret reason?"

Daddy was stopping the car at the pony ring, and he looked over at her. "A secret reason?" he asked, and he frowned.

"Yes. There's a secret reason why Grampa calls me Princess, and why Ella calls me Little Ella, and why the milkman calls me Curlytop, and —oh, all those names. Mommy knows the secret reason."

"It must be Mommy's secret, then," Daddy said. "Come on, out!"

Eileen ran over to the ponies. One of them put his nose in her hand, but her hand was empty. Eileen rubbed him right in the middle of his nose,

21

and he liked that. The man who ran the pony
ring came over.

"Is that the one you want, Sport?" he asked.

"It sure is." Eileen climbed up on the pony
and then she said, "My name's not Sport. My
name's Eileen."

"That's right, Sport," the man said, and he
slapped the pony so he would start around the
ring.

Eileen felt about ten feet tall when she rode that pony, and she hated to stop. She was glad when she saw Daddy give the man another quarter. The man waved her on, and the pony went around the ring three more times. Then she had to get off.

"See you again, Sport," the man called after her as she walked toward the car. Eileen just waved good-bye.

When Eileen was putting the cottage cheese on the salad plates for dinner, she told Mother about the pony man who called her Sport.

"Does he do it for that secret reason?" she asked.

"Well, maybe—just a little bit, anyway," Mother said.

"Will you tell me the reason now?"

"Oh, goodness, you give me no peace!" Mother laughed. "Yes, I'll tell you when you're ready for bed. Now scoot and call Daddy for dinner. Thank you, Missy."

25

Missy! There was another name, one that Mother called her. Eileen scooted and called her father. She was hungry and she wanted her dinner, but she was almost in a hurry to get to bed to hear that secret reason for all the names.

Mother sat down on Eileen's bed. She smoothed the sheet and she smoothed the pillow-case and she smoothed Eileen's hair.

"The reason, Mommy! The secret reason!"

"All right, honey. Maybe you'll be disappointed, because you've really made this into a big thing. Somebody told me this a long, long time ago, and when you are an old, old lady, you may tell it to someone else. It's something so true we'll go on saying it, maybe forever."

"But what is it, Mommy?"

"Now, just a minute. Remember, no story tonight, because tomorrow is Ella's birthday, and you'll be staying up late at her house. We'll have just the reason tonight, and that may give you a

lot to think about. It's the reason for all those
names—Curlytop and Princess and Sport and
what else?"

"I-ee and Little Ella and—"

"Missy!" They said it together, and they
laughed.

"And this is the reason," Mother said. "The child who is loved has many names."

"The child who is loved has many names," Eileen repeated. "But my name is Eileen."

"Yes, but all the people who love you and who think you are special give you a name that is special, too. Even people like the milkman think of nicknames that suit you. So you have many names. Lots of us love you. And that's it. Good night."

Mother turned out the light and left the room. Eileen lay with only a crack of light under the door of her room, thinking about what her mother had said. "The child who is loved has many names." That sounded nice, and so did the names. She said them again, just to herself. "Curlytop . . . Princess . . . Little Ella . . . I-ee . . . Tiger . . . Sport . . . Missy." Then she snuggled down in her bed and fell asleep.